Moose
is Loose on the
Palouse

Moose is Loose on the Palouse

by Seema Jot Kaur pictures by Chris Shanahan

BLUE IRIS JOY

To Bob

"So es das Liben"

With much love and blessings my three sons and beloved husband who have gifted me with motherhood and the best family EVER!

To the Readers

Embrace your uniqueness; love it and leverage it!

"Be yourself; as everyone else is already taken."

- Oscar Wilde

There once was a moose who was loose on the Palouse! He liked to roam free and just be. He took his sweet time and did his own thing. "Chi!Chi!Chi!"

He wandered and pondered and sometimes sauntered into town. This would cause quite a stir!

"What is a moose doing loose on the Palouse?!" the townspeople would exclaim. Moose gave it no mind and wandered away.

One day, not long ago, Moose decided to head into town to get some dessert for his brood; they all loved chocolate mousse with whipped cream!

Along the way he encountered Blue Jay who jeered and gurgled.

"Moose, what are you doing on the Palouse?"

"Well, Blue Jay, I am enjoying the green rolling hills."

"Makes sense, it is beautiful here!" exclaimed Blue Jay.

Moose kept meandering to town beside the river. He could hear it flowing and see an occasional fish jump and splash. As Moose crossed over the river and stepped onto the riverbank, Squirrel came bounding down a tree and chittered. "Moose, what are your doing on the Palouse?"

"Well, Squirrel," responded Moose, "I am here with my wife, Deer, and my three sons."

Squirrel replied, "Of course, the Palouse is full of bountiful, rolling fields." And then he bounded off as quickly as he came.

Moose now walked for a mile and was almost to town when Butterfly fluttered by. She paused long enough to say, "Moose, you have made it to the Palouse! So glad you are here."

"Thank you!" said Moose "I am indeed happy to be here!" Butterfly fluttered off.

Once Moose was in town, he clip-clomped into the general store with an excitement in his step and a smile on his face.

Phil, the shopkeeper, gave him a sideways stare. "What is a moose doing loose on the Palouse? We don't usually see YOUR kind here!"

Moose replied, "My family and I came here from British Columbia to grow wheat and live a joyful, carefree life on the gold and green rolling hills of the Palouse. I am looking for chocolate mousse and whipped cream! Do you have any?"

"That is a STRANGE request, especially coming from a moose. It is just about as strange as you." Phil said with a stomp. "We DO NOT have chocolate mousse, and even if we did, I would not sell it to YOU!"

Moose looked down, his antlers feeling especially heavy. His heart said, 'You don't belong, you don't fit in.'

He sadly nudged the screen door open and began to make his way home - mousse-less.

He walked past his favorite lime-green willow tree and paused to think for a moment.

He decided Phil couldn't see others for who they really are and that, someday very soon, even a moose loose on the Palouse would be accepted and loved!

As Moose crossed over the stream right before his house, Butterfly fluttered by and observed Moose with a down - trodden look on his face. "Moose, what is the trouble?"

Moose replied, "I am sad and disappointed because I couldn't find any mousse for my family and Phil doesn't seem to like me."

"Ahh, Moose, you are wonderful and have an extraordinary and beautiful family. That is your focus. Pay Phil no mind and everything will work out. He doesn't understand that we are all special in our own way."

"Being unique is AMAZING!"

Moose nodded. This time his antlers didn't feel as heavy as earlier. His heart was happier, too! Butterfly fluttered off just as Moose opened the door to his cabin.

The second Moose opened the door, he was astounded and ecstatic. Deer and his three sons were cooking chocolate mousse on the wood stove and whipping cream!

The cabin was filled with love, laughter and levity.

What a delightful and precious moment Moose had walked into. He knew it was going to be another fantastic night with his brilliant herd—and a tasty one, too!

"Daaaaad! Dad! Daddy!" his three sons cheered and gave him a furry antler bump. Deer pecked his moosey cheek.

He knew he was truly home, and nothing else mattered. His mission was crystal clear. Wander the Palouse, gather food for his brood (maybe not mousse), and love them with all his might!

What mattered was his family; that was his destiny. Moose knew he was a GOOD soul. So the next time you see a moose loose on the Palouse, you will know he is taking his time and doing his thing.

What better place to be than wandering loose on the Palouse?

"Chi! Chi! Chi!"

Seema Jot Kaur

Education and literacy are important to Seema Jot Kaur. She has been writing since she could hold a pen. When she was six years old, she began writing letters to her grandparents, aunts, and uncles. She also drafted poems in her Hello Kitty journal. Seema Jot received her Bachelors of English degree from the University of Washington and recently completed her MBA. She has realized there is a need for a path to help children navigate the intense pressures of growing up and embracing the "you" of you, even and especially if it doesn't seem to fit what society, family members or others in the community expect you to be. In addition, Seema Jot is passionate about conservation and keeping the planet healthy for future generations. A portion of the sale of each book will be donated to the Nature Conservancy. Seema Jot has raised three wonderful, unique, and amazing sons and now has the pleasure of two beautiful grandchildren, with whom she loves reading stories to and hanging out with at the beach building sandcastles and searching for wonderful beach treasures. She has always been an avid reader and over the years has created an entire library of books for her children, which now her grandchildren are benefitting from. She spent a short time as a preschool teacher post-retirement and her two favorite things to do with the children were to read them amazing stories and do yoga with them. The rest of her time is taking sunset walks with her husband and planning vacations to new and unknown destinations (including the Palouse) as well as tried and true favorite locales. To learn more about Seema Jot and her children's and adult yoga classes, aromatherapy and oracle card readings visit her website at www.blueirisjoy.com or follow her on Instagram @blueirisjoy.

Chris Shanahan

Co-founder of Unleash Creatives (unleashcreatives.com), Chris Shanahan is a graphic artist with a focus on serving writers, publishers and the literary world in general. His studio focuses on both fine and commercial arts including commissioned acrylic, oil and mixed media paintings, including Murals, technical drawings using traditional media, computer graphics & design, typography, data visualization, infographics, business presentation design and brand & logo design.

Jen Knox

Based in the Midwest, Jen Knox is a writer and writing coach. She spends her days teaching, practicing yoga, hiking, and spending time with her beautiful family. Jen is the author of Mindful Fiction: How to Write a Short Story in 10 Days and the short story collections After the Gazebo (Pen/Faulkner nominee), The Glass City (Prize Americana winner) and Resolutions: A Family in Stories. Her stories have been featured in textbooks, classrooms, and both online and print publications around the world, such as Chicago Tribune, The Bombay Literary Review, The Saturday Evening Post and NPR Online. Jen founded and co-owns Unleash Creatives, a creativity consultancy, where she coaches writers from idea to publication. Connect with her here: jenknox.com

Emily Hutton

Hello friends my name is Emily Hutton, and I'm a graphic designer. My main goal in life was to find a career that brings me joy everyday, luckily graphic design has created that outlet for me. I hope to create a pleasing aesthetic that not only captures the viewer's eye, but allows them to have an experience and make their own personal connections through design as well. Please give me a follow @real_space_case on Instagram or email me huttonemily28@gmail.com for inquires.

CPSIA information can be obtained at www.ICGtesting.com
Printed in the USA
LVIW010055240321
682262LV00001B/4